BOG HOLLOW BOYS

Bog Hollow Boys is published by
Stone Arch Books, a Capstone Imprint
1710 Roe Crest Drive
North Mankato, Minnesota 56003
www.mycapstone.com

Library of Congress Cataloging-in-Publication Data
is available at the Library of Congress website.

ISBN: 978-1-4965-4056-0 (library binding)
ISBN: 978-1-4965-4060-7 (eBook pdf)

Summary:
Nellie must find her lost pet snake with the help of the Bog Hollow Boys and prove
that snakes aren't as dangerous as they are often made out to be.

Designer: Ted Williams
Editor: Nate LeBoutillier

Printed and bound in Canada.
010010S17

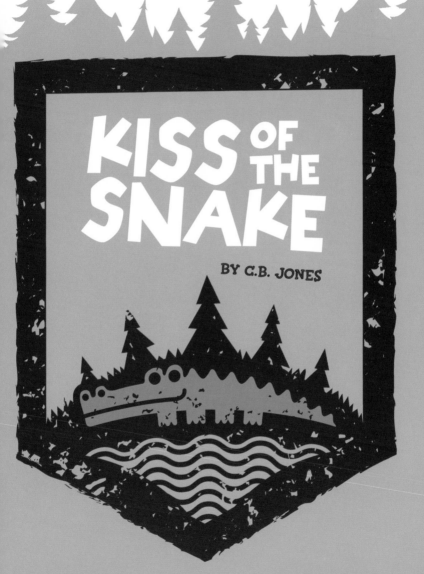

KISS OF THE SNAKE

BY C.B. JONES

STONE ARCH BOOKS
a capstone imprint

TABLE OF CONTENTS

The **BOG HOLLOW BOYS** vow

to protect, serve, and nurture the animals in and around B.H.S.P. (Bog Hollow State Park). No animal is too small, large, cute, ugly, slimy, furry, feathered, stinky, or dirty for their attention. Bog Hollow Boys to the rescue!

AUSTIN "ACE" FINCH
Age: 12
Skills: Leadership, Grit, Birds

NELLIE TIBBITS
Age: 12
Skills: Smarts, Sass, Snakes

DARYL "DA SNAKE" TATE
Age: 12
Skills: Jokes, Wrestling, Pets

ETHAN "EL GATOR" FINCH
Age: 10
Skills: Tagging Along, Wrestling, Fish

RANGER FINCH

Father of Austin and Ethan and the warden of B.H.S.P.

DR. TIBBITS

Mother of new girl Nellie and famous herpetologist

MS. FINCH

Mother of Austin and Ethan, P.E. teacher, & wrestling coach

MISS DENISE

Granny of Daryl Tate, lover of cats, & outstanding cook

THE MANLEYS

Bad boy brothers who are always up to no good

WILLIE AND BUD

B.H.S.P. junior rangers who keep a watchful eye on the park

CHAPTER ONE

OUT ON THE TRAIL

It was the first day of summer break for the Bog Hollow Boys, and it was raining. They stood beside their four-wheelers at the trailhead of Bog Hollow State Park and watched the puddles along the trail get bigger and muddier.

In early summer in South Georgia, rain often came twice a day—once in the afternoon and once in late evening. When it wasn't raining, sun would turn everything into a gnatty, sticky sauna. Early dawn and late dusk were really the only two times to be outside without getting heat stroke.

Austin, Ethan, Daryl, and Nellie were excited to be out of school. They each had a Bog Hollow State Park four-wheeler. They were ready to hit the trails, even in the rain.

Daryl was lovingly patting the seat of his ride. "Boy, oh boy," he kept saying. "She's a beaut."

Nellie adjusted the straps of her helmet and pulled it over her head. "I'm cool with safety," she said. "But I hate what this helmet is doing to my Mohawk."

Austin scoffed. "Always worried about your hair."

Nellie stuck her tongue out at him.

Ranger Finch said, "That's enough." He lifted his youngest son, Ethan, off the four-wheeler. "Okay, y'all," he said. "What's our first rule of four-wheeler safety? Before we even get on the ATV, we . . . "

Ethan wriggled out of his father's grasp. "We go down the checklist!" he said.

"That's right," said Ranger Finch. The rain had let up a little and was coming down in more of a mist, but droplets still ran off his ranger hat. He paced back and forth in front of the four, ticking items off on his fingers. "Boots? Check. Helmets? Check. Gas and oil? Check."

Like a drill sergeant, Austin thought.

Ranger Finch motioned to Daryl. "Mr. Tate," said the ranger. "Why are your sleeves and pant legs rolled up?"

Daryl panted. "It's hot out here, even in the rain," he said. "Even for a cold-blooded snake like myself. You

know, when I dreamt last night about racin' this ATV — I mean *ridin'* — I was wearin' my usual, cooler outfit, not this bunch of sweaty safety clothes. And also, our ATVs were, like, matchin' our outfits. Even, Nellie's snake, Red, had a helmet on. And also, I was doin' flips and sidekicks. Which I know we definitely ain't goin' to be doin'. Like, definitely not."

Ranger Finch said, "Are you finished, Daryl?"

Austin glared at Daryl.

"Yes, sir," said Daryl. "I'm ready to be real safe on this here ATV, even if I'm sweatin' and stuff."

"Pull down those sleeves and tuck them into your gloves," said Ranger Finch. "Same with the pants."

Dr. Tibbits, Nellie's mother and the park's resident herpetologist, had joined Ranger Finch. She shoook her head. "Nellie," she said. "Is your helmet on tight?"

"As tight as it goes," said Nellie.

"Last thing," said Ranger Finch. "I see y'all eyeing those puddles. But if you take these machines through water and flood 'em, you'll be workin' double shifts at the new visitor's center to pay repairs."

The ranger jerked a thumb over his shoulder at the building behind him. A banner above the door read, *COME SEE THE DEADLIEST SNAKES OF SOUTHEAST GEORGIA*. All the S's were drawn in to look like snakes. It was the the joint project of Ranger Finch and Dr. Tibbits.

Daryl said, "Hey, Dr. Tibbs. How come that sign don't say to come *wrestle* the the deadliest snakes?" He rolled up his sleeves and slapped Larry and Roger as he spoke. Larry and Roger were the snakes he magic-markered onto his arms each morning.

"Roll those sleeves back down," said Austin. "I want to get out on the trails."

Dr. Tibbits said, "We're trying to educate people about snakes. We're trying to help both the people and the snakes from having to fight each other."

"Yeah," said Nellie. "Not all snakes are as popular as Red." Red, Nellie's pet corn snake, lay curled in the transport cage strapped to the back of her ATV.

"Don't you let Red out of her case when you're out on the trail," said Dr. Tibbits. She sighed and turned to Ranger Finch. "Shall we let them go?"

Ranger Finch nodded.

Austin turned on the choke of his four-wheeler and cranked the engine. The machine growled to life. He kept both his hands on the handlebars and pressed with his foot to shift into first gear.

At the sudden noise, Dr. Tibbits winced.

"Remember," Ranger Finch shouted. "No speedin'!" But no one seemed to hear him. Daryl let out a whoop. Then the Bog Hollow Boys roared off, leaving a cloud of red dust behind them.

CHAPTER TWO

TREE SNAKES

They had the early morning trail all to themselves. The scrub oaks and cypress lining the trail were draped in Spanish moss.

Austin kept a wary eye on the lowest tree branches. He remembered that Dr. Tibbits had warned that with the recent hard rain, snakes would be seeking high ground.

Austin wasn't *afraid* of snakes, exactly. But he preferred to keep his distance. He looked at Nellie's four-wheeler, a few yards up the trail. That crazy girl and her pet snake were puttering along the dirt road.

For someone who'd never ridden alone before, Nellie was doing fine. Better than fine, actually. She couldn't stop grinning. The ATV went over a little dip in the trail, and she caught air.

"How you doing back there, Austin?" she yelled. She knew he couldn't hear her, but she shouted it anyway.

Daryl was talking softly to his four-wheeler as he drove along. "That's nice, girl," he kept saying. "Nice and easy, nice and easy." He eased his hand off the brakes. "Nice and easy."

Ethan made *vroom-vroom* noises as he drove along.

When they reached the first trail pull-off, they killed the engines.

"Whoo!" said Nellie. She pulled off her helmet and fluffed up the spikes of her hair. "That's fun."

"Anyone see any tree snakes yet?" said Ethan. "Chomp, chomp!"

"Snakes in trees!" Daryl whistled. His eyes darted from branch to branch.

Austin was less stoked. "Snakes in trees," he mumbled to himself. "Great."

"They don't even have arms," Ethan said. "How can snakes climb trees?"

"It's called *concertina locomotion*," Austin said. "They grab onto the tree with one part of their body and pull themselves up with the other parts. It's like a Slinky in reverse."

Austin turned back to Nellie. "You ain't the only one who knows about snakes."

Nellie said, "How you gonna work at the snake education center if you're scared of snakes, Ace?" She grinned and patted Red's case. "You want to hold Red? Get some practice?"

Austin said, "No thanks. I'm all set."

"More like all *chicken*," said Nellie.

"Da Snake hates to interrupt this lovers' spat," said Daryl. Both Austin and Nellie glared at him. "But does anyone else hear something crashing this way?" He cupped a hand around the outside of his helmet, where the ear would be.

Austin heard it too. The low rumbling was coming closer. He could hear tree branches snapping and puddles splashing. Whoever it was, they weren't staying on the trail.

He narrowed his eyes.

His suspicions were confirmed when he saw the figure break through the trees and skid up the trail. The rider was dressed in head-to-toe camouflage, but Austin recognized the chubby frame. "A Manley," he muttered.

"There goes the neighborhood," said Daryl. He slapped his arms. "You want me to handle this, Ace?"

Austin removed his helmet and held up a hand. The Manley skidded to a stop and sprayed red mud all over Austin.

"What do you want?" Austin said. He wiped mud from his face.

He couldn't tell which Manley it was — Hobie or

Hunter. It didn't matter. Both had been Austin's sworn enemies as long as he could remember.

"I need your help," said the Manley. "Hobie's stuck in the mud, and we got a sick dog we're trying to get to your mama. The snake lady."

Nellie scoffed. "You expect us to believe you? We're not falling for any of your dumb tricks."

"Hurry," panted Hunter. "Something is really wrong with Bubba."

"Da Snake is a snake," said Daryl. "Not an idiot."

"Fine!" shouted Hunter. "I guess y'all animal lovers are just gonna let a helpless dog die." He slammed down his face shield and revved the four-wheeler into gear. Then he raced back the way he had come.

Austin sighed. "Okay," he said finally. "Follow me."

"You believe that joker, Ace?" Daryl said.

"I don't know if I believe him," said Austin. He wrestled his helmet back on and waved his hand. "But we might as well keep riding."

CHAPTER THREE

SWAMPED

The rain couldn't make up its mind. It drizzled, then stopped, then started spitting again. The humidity grew as the sun crept above the foggy mist.

Austin sighed as he navigated the four-wheeler along the path Hunter had made. Ranger Finch wasn't going to be too happy about them messing up the plants along the trail.

He could almost hear his daddy now: "There's a trail because the last thing I need is to go rescue some dummy wallered out in a mud hole."

If there was one thing Ranger Finch really hated, it was yahoos going off-trail and wrecking his park.

Nellie pulled up alongside him and waved. She pointed ahead and gunned her engine. Whatever she saw, she wanted to get to it in a hurry.

It was the Manleys, all right. Hunter and Hobie had a four-wheeler buried in a thick marsh along the swamp. Hunter was perched behind handlebars of the stuck four-wheeler. Hobie squatted on the back, rocking to try to get traction. The wheels spun in place.

Mud sprayed the other four-wheeler with a stream of filth. Bubba the bulldog was slumped on the back. He weakly lapped the splatter on his muzzle.

Austin and Nellie stopped along the last inches of firm ground between the Manleys and where the marshes began. "A fine mess you've gotten yourselves into this time," Nellie said. "From the looks of it, you boys tried to take a shortcut?"

"It's Bubba," Hobie said. "Snake bit him. We were tryin' to get him over to Dr. Tibbits fast as we could."

"I already told ya," Hunter said. "We were trying to get him to your ma."

Nellie and Austin both squinted for a better look. Neither could tell what condition the dog was in with all the mud that Hunter and Hobie had sprayed on him.

"What kind of snake was it?" Austin yelled. He'd hopped off his ATV and was ready to wade in after them.

"A big snake," Hobie said.

Nellie rolled her yes. "What kind of big snake?" she yelled. "What'd it look like?"

"I don't know," Hobie yelled back. "We were gettin' our four-wheelers out of the shed. It was dark."

Austin reached for the rope that secured Red's transport case to the back of Nellie's four-wheeler and pulled it from around the case. "Ethan," he shouted. "Go get me the biggest tree branches you can find. And watch out for snakes!"

"Don't you let Red get out," said Nellie.

"I won't," said Austin. "But I need this rope because I'm guessing these two ding-dongs don't have a safety kit on them. Nellie, go get that doggie some help," Austin said. He nodded at his four-wheeler. "We'll get these boys unstuck."

Nellie grabbed Bubba. The dog panted short quick breaths. Nellie felt warm drool running down her arm.

She hoisted him into her lap and started up Austin's four-wheeler. "Don't go dying on me now, doggie," she whispered in Bubba's ear. "Just hang on."

To Austin, she shouted, "You take care of my snake!" Then she was gone, crashing back down the trail to the visitor's center.

"Da Snake got his snake eye on Red," shouted Daryl.

Austin unwound the rope and handed one end to Hunter. "Why don't you make yourself useful," he told him. "Tie this off as low as you can get it up under the grill. Give it the old sailor's knot."

"I don't know how to tie knots," said Hobie.

"He don't even know how to tie his shoes the right way," said Hunter.

Daryl said, "How is it possible that you two meatheads have made it this far in life without learning to do anything for yourselves?"

Austin waded in further, almost to his waist. He gritted his teeth and tried not to think about snakes in the swamp. Instead, he tied the rope to the front of the stuck four-wheeler.

Ethan brought back some branches.

Austin pointed at the stuck tires. "Put 'em under the tires for traction," he said. He jumped onto the four-wheeler and revved the engine. Gears whined as he pushed the throttle.

"Daryl," he shouted. "I need some more weight up on this. Jump up."

Daryl climbed up on the stuck four-wheeler.

Austin gunned it again. This time, the wheels caught. The ATV jumped backward and onto the trail.

"Now then," Austin panted. He got off the Manley's filthy four-wheeler. "Let's go see about that dog."

"Hold up, Ace," said Daryl. He pointed at the transport case with Red inside it. "Don't be leaving anyone behind."

"Great," muttered Austin. He balanced the snake case on his lap and gritted his teeth. "This morning just keeps getting better and better."

CHAPTER FOUR

SNAKEBIT

Nellie drove as fast as she dared toward the ranger station with Bubba. Both were drenched and caked with mud when she pulled up.

Inside the station, Dr. Tibbits, Mr. Manley, and Ranger Finch were measuring a counter. Nellie and Bubba barged in with junior ranger Bud a step behind.

"*Help,*" Nellie rasped. "*Snakebite . . . Bubba . . .*"

Dr. Tibbits grabbed the anti-venom kit. "What kind of snake was it?" Dr. Tibbits asked. She pulled on latex gloves and a mask.

Bubba was on his side. He panted a million breaths a minute and drooled all over. Both eyes had swollen shut. His nose was as red as Nellie's spiky hair.

"My bet's copperhead or cottonmouth," Nellie said. "Hobie said it was in the back of their shed."

"What's happened to my boys?" asked Mr. Manley.

Nellie gathered up all the breath she could. "They're fine," she said. "They got stuck in those swamps out your way. But the Finch boys and Daryl are there, helping them out."

Mr. Manley let out a sigh that turned into a snarl. Then without another word, he stormed out into the rain. A moment later they heard him start a four-wheeler and gun it and ride off.

Ranger Finch pointed at Bud. "Get me the mule ready," he said. "Y'all got this under control?" he asked Dr. Tibbits. He was already heading out the door before Dr. Tibbits or Nellie could say one way or another.

Nellie waited a minute after it was just the two of them. She stroked the dog's quivering back and watched her mom as she injected the dog's muzzle.

"You got this, right, Mom?" Nellie asked. "You're not going let their dog die from a little snake bite, are you?"

"I'm doing what I can, Nellie," Dr. Tibbits said. Bubba's breathing had slowed down a little, but his eyes were still swollen shut and his fat tongue was still lolling out.

Bubba's smile is kind of scary, Nellie thought. She hated the way furry animals smiled when they got hurt or sick.

"Call the vet just in case," Dr. Tibbits said, watching her daughter tear up. "They'll be able to take over once we've got his swelling down."

Nellie sniffled. She reached up and scratched the dog behind its floppy bulldog ears. "After all I did for you, you better survive this, you big furball," she said.

She knew that if Bubba didn't survive, Mr. Manley would round up every last snake in the county.

CHAPTER FIVE

HUNTING

The anti-venom and Dr. Tibbits' quick action worked. Within a couple days Bubba was back to playing — or fighting, anyway — with Miss Stella, their cat.

The Manleys, though, held a grudge. Their father accused the Tibbitses of endangering everyone with all their snakes. In particular, the boys didn't seem to like Nellie's pet snake, Red. And it definitely didn't matter to them that all the snakes for the new exhibit were straight from Bog Hollow State Park. Or that Nellie was the one who'd saved Bubba.

The way Hunter and Hobie saw it, their life was under attack. First, they almost lost Bubba. Then, they lost the use of their four-wheelers. And to top it off, they had to go back to B.H.S.P. for Ranger Finch's new mandatory snake safety class.

Well, if they had to take the class if they wanted to ride their four-wheelers in Bog Hollow State Park, anyway. Which they did, of course.

Hunter showed up with a garden hoe strapped across his back. "From now on, I come prepared," Hunter said. "From now on, I am the Snake Hunter." He sneered at Daryl and Nellie when he said that.

Daryl immediately dropped his bike and yanked off his shirt. "Oh, you think you're a big snake hunter, now, huh?" he said. He slapped his biceps where he'd markered on his snakes. "Let's see what old Roger and Larry have to say about that."

Hobie rode up on his bike in coveralls, leather gloves, and snakeskin boots. He could hardly stay upright as he pedaled. Sweat drenched him, and he looked ready to pass out.

"Got to have my snake boots," Hobie said. He walked around like a chubby toddler trying to steady its legs. "My daddy bought 'em for me."

"You know those ain't snake boots," Austin said. "Those there are snake*skin* boots. They ain't gonna protect you from nothing."

Daryl and Ethan cracked up.

"All right now," Ranger Finch said. "Don't everybody need to pile on poor old Hobie here. He's had a rough go." He cleared his throat. "So, we got ourselves a little field trip here today."

The kids all put their heads down and groaned.

"Field trip?" Hobie whined. "What for?"

"To learn something," Ranger Finch said. He turned to nod at Nellie.

Nellie said, "We need to make sure we're all prepared for our next snake run-in."

Ranger Finch threw a leg up and over his bicycle. "We're headed to Dr. Tibbit's lab at the college. Roll out, team."

By the time they biked to the college, the Manley boys had nearly kicked the bucket. Daryl and Ethan were tired, too, but they didn't show it. Everyone perked up when they got to campus and entered the air-conditioned science building.

Dr. Tibbits' lab had fifteen different species of snakes native to the swamps of South Georgia. She had eastern indigos and yellow-bellied king snakes. She had copperheads and cottonmouths. She had harmless garters and black racers. She had diamondbacks and timber rattlers. She had an eastern hognose and a southern hognose.

Once, she had a corn snake named Red. But she'd given Red to Nellie. So she'd replaced it with another. Nellie had named that one Orange.

Dr. Tibbits maintained a population of dangerous snakes. But she also had other snakes that people often confused with venomous snakes.

That morning, she pointed to two snake habitats. Both snakes had rings of black, red, and yellow.

"One of these is a scarlet king and harmless," she said. "And one of them is a venomous coral snake. Can anyone tell me which one is which?"

"Trick question," Daryl said. "Both of them snakes is the same snake."

"Our daddy says, *When in doubt kill 'em both*," Hunter said.

"Yep," said Hobie. "Let nature sort it out."

"Man killin' snake ain't nature!" yelled Daryl.

"Yes it is!" said Hobie. "It's the law of the jungle!"

Daryl slapped his forehead with his palm.

Dr. Tibbits sighed. "Nellie," she said, "can you tell these boys the difference?"

Before Nellie could answer, Austin blurted it out. "Red on yellow," he said, "kill a fellow. Red on black, friend of Jack."

"Very good, Austin," Dr. Tibbits said. "You really do know your snakes."

Hobie said, "Riddle me this, ma'am: what kind of snake bit Bubba?"

"What did it look like?" Dr. Tibbits asked.

"Real big," Hobie said. "Otherwise old Bubba would've been able to bite it back."

Dr. Tibbits moved to the copperhead terrarium. "Most likely it was one of these," she said. "It's a fact that copperheads are responsible for most snakebites in the country. And they like to hide in dark places like a shed."

"Didn't it look more like this one?" Hunter said. He was pointing at the compartment for the corn snake. He was pointing at Orange.

"Yeah," Hobie said. "That's the one."

"No," Nellie shouted. "That's not the one." She knew full well that they were trying to get under her skin. It was working. "That's a corn snake," she said. "They eat rats. And they're not even poisonous."

"It's okay," Dr. Tibbits said. "I'm sure Hunter and Hobie are just a little confused. It's easy to confuse corn snakes and copperheads. Their patterns can be very similar."

"No," Hobie said. "I'm pretty sure now. That's the one that got Bubba. I'd recognize that snake anywhere." He kept throwing glances at Hunter, who in turn kept throwing glances at Nellie.

"In the dark like that," said Dr. Tibbits, more forcefully, "it would be easy to make a mistake."

"Nope," Hobie said. He pursed his lips. "I'm almost a hundred percent sure it was this one."

CHAPTER SIX

OUT OF THE CAGE

The new snake education visitor's center at Bog Hollow State Park was almost done. Dr. Tibbits and Ranger Finch had worked nights and weekends. The empty terrariums were all set up and awaiting the snakes.

Dr. Tibbits wanted to let the Bog Hollow Boys take a private tour first. And of course no one could tell Daryl no when it came to snakes. But she could tell Nellie was still shaken about the Manleys.

Austin stood in the doorway of the center. His arms were folded up into his armpits, and his chin rested on his chest.

Nellie was doing her best to ignore Austin. Ever since her mom and his dad had started this snake project, his negative attitude spread to everything.

"Don't you think it's a little dangerous?" he said. "Putting all these snakes together like this?"

"Snakes smell fear," Nellie said. "Red can literally taste all the adrenalin you're pumping."

"You think she can taste how bored I am, havin' to stand here and listen to all this?" Austin said.

"Don't pay no attention to, Ace, here," Daryl told Nellie. "Old Ace, he's jealous that y'all ain't buildin' an aviary for his birds instead. Now take Red out. Let's see that beauty."

"Take it easy, D," Nellie whispered.

She gently lifted Red from the transport case and laid her on a limb in an empty terrarium. "She's already a little spooked to be out here. Snakes don't exactly react well to new environments like this."

Thunder rattled the whole building. The lights flickered off, then back on. Then they flickered off again and stayed off.

"Hey, whoa, whoa, whoa," Daryl called out. "Y'all turn the lights back on. Da Snake don't do too well in the pitch dark."

"Ooh!" Ethan said with a giggle. "It's the ghost of El Gator come to haunt Da Snake."

"Cut it out, there, Gator Bait," Daryl said with a crack in his voice.

Nellie felt the top of the terrarium nervously. "Red," she said, tapping the glass. "You all right in there? Can you hear me? It's going to be okay, Red."

A flashlight appeared in the doorway. "Everybody just take it easy," said the voice of Ranger Finch. His light bounced from glass tank to glass tank. It settled, finally, on Nellie's squinting face.

Austin mock shrieked. "Oh, no, the snakes!" he said. "They're eatin' Nellie's head!"

Everyone grumbled, moaned, or booed at Austin in unison.

"Okay, everybody just take it real easy," Ranger Finch said. He went from face to face with the spotlight to make sure that all the kids were accounted for.

Dr. Tibbits found her way in, too. She had her own flashlight and turned it on Nellie.

"Where is she?" Dr. Tibbits asked.

"Where's who?" Ranger Finch said.

"Red, my snake," Nellie said. "She was just here. Right as I put her in this tank, the lights went out. But now I don't see her." Her voice was getting higher and higher.

Ranger Finch and Dr. Tibbits ran their flashlights along the tanks again.

Daryl began to feel his way around in the dark. "Here Reddy-red-red!" he called. "C'mere, girl!"

"Shh," Ranger Finch whispered. "If we listen, we might hear her move."

Dr. Tibbits found her daughter in the dark. "It's okay," she whispered in Nellie's ear. "It's just a little power outage. We'll find Red."

None of them noticed that Austin has slipped out the back and put as much distance between him and the missing snake as possible.

CHAPTER SEVEN

THE GREAT ESCAPE

Twenty-four hours — a whole day — passed. They still hadn't found Red. The only clue they had was a back door left ajar.

"It wasn't you, was it?" everyone said to everyone else. And everyone said it wasn't them, including Austin. He wasn't ready to admit to anyone that he'd probably let Nellie's snake escape. No telling where Red could be hiding now: in the swamp, bogs, ponds, or creek.

To make things worse, it'd poured rain all night. Eagle Creek had overflown and flooded.

Ranger Finch called off an extensive search. "Too risky," he'd said. "It's too wet out here. We'll find a copperhead trying to stay dry and get hurt."

It was still raining the next day when the kids reconvened at B.H.S.P.. This time, Austin had called for reinforcement in the form of his mother, Ms. Finch. Even though she'd be up in arms — she was always preaching about the dangers of the park, especialled since she and Ranger Finch divorced — Austin figured Nellie could use the support.

"Well," Ms. Finch said, pacing back and forth, her whistle dangling from her lips. The end of the whistle wiggled out of the corner of her mouth whenever she talked.

Even though wrestling season was over, she was still in coach mode. "This right here, this is what we've been preparing for all along. We shall leave no stone unturned, no rotten log unkicked. No rain nor mud shall deter us from finding our man."

"You mean snake, right?" Daryl said. "And isn't Red a female snake?"

Ms. Finch stuck out her chin in Daryl's face. "Does this seem like a good time for jokes, Daryl? Did I ask if any of y'all had any silly questions to waste our time with?"

Daryl shook his head. "No ma'am," he said with a sniffle. "Da Snake was just a little confused."

Ms. Finch straightened herself on her bike. "This is no time to be questioning our mission, people. This young lady's best friend in the whole world has gone missing. It's up to all of us mud-buggers to find him."

"Her," Ethan corrected.

"Are you questioning my — " Ms. Finch started.

But at that same moment three important things happened. First, it thundered hard and loud, which rumbled through every tree in the bog. Second, the rain went from a hard rain to a full-on downpour. And third, the Manley boys showed up on their four-wheelers. They were carrying a garden hoe and a pitchfork. They had Bubba bundled up in a doggy raincoat. He looked to be fully healed from his snakebite.

"We wanna help," Hunter said.

"Yeah," said Hobie. "We felt bad about blamin' Bubba's snakebite on Red."

Nellie craned her neck and squinted through the rain. She eyed the garden hoe and the pitchfork. Her nostrils were flared, and Austin, Daryl, and Ethan could see the steam coming out of them.

Austin shook his head. So did Ethan and Daryl.

It was Daryl who spoke up. "Nah," he yelled through the rain and wind. "We don't want y'all's help. Y'all done quite enough, thank you."

"What'd you say?" Hunter yelled back. He cupped his ear to the wind and made out as if he couldn't hear with the rain and the idling of their four-wheelers.

Before Daryl or any of the others could say no again, Ms. Finch had the final word.

"Well, come on, then," she yelled and waved them over. "We'll take all the eyes and ears we can get."

"Yeah," Austin muttered. "I bet they'll be real helpful if they get to Red first."

CHAPTER EIGHT

TOGETHER

It was a full-on search party. Junior rangers Bud and Willie, Daryl's granny Miss Denise, and Mr. Manley and his sons were helping scour every nook and cranny of the park.

Ranger Finch and Dr. Tibbits focused their efforts on taking apart the snake education center. They dug out the burrowing holes and removed the climbing logs and swimming holes. Still no sign of Red.

Miss Denise set up a warming station in Ranger Finch's office. She brought blankets and soup for the drenched search team. Bud and Willie cleaned out the storage sheds — carefully.

Mr. Manley had brought his tools and went to town disassembling all the display cases he'd helped build for the new visitors' center. Miss Denise and Ms. Finch even set up a little burner and made jambalaya.

On a dinner break, something caught Austin's eye. Every so often Ranger Finch would pat Dr. Tibbits on the back. And they were whispering to each other like school kids.

It disgusted Austin so much that he went outside. He leaned up against a wall and tried to take the situation all in. He attempted to take a deep breath but couldn't. At that moment, Nellie appeared.

"They're gonna end up together," Nellie said. "You know that, right?"

"Who?" Austin said with a snort.

"It's pretty sickening, actually," Nellie said. There was a tired quality to her voice. It was like she'd given up on finding Red ever again.

"What is?" Austin said.

"Your dad," Nellie said. "My mom. He's all she talks about these days. *That Ranger Finch is so nice*, she tells me. *That Ranger Finch has been so helpful with the snake exhibit.*"

Austin's stomach dropped.

Nellie sighed. "We used to talk about snakes all the time, you know? Now it's *Ranger Finch* this and *Ranger Finch* that."

"My daddy," Austin said, his eyes flashing, "would *never* date your mama."

"It's already happening," Nellie said.

Austin stared straight ahead.

Nellie sighed. "You think I want this?"

Austin didn't respond.

"Listen, Ace. I get it," Nellie said. "I've had to do things I didn't want. I never wanted to move down here. Up north, I was the weirdo girl, but at least I had a couple friends."

"Let me assure you," Austin said. "You're still the weirdo girl."

"Thanks," Nellie said.

"Well, what do you expect?" Austin said. "Look at your hair and the way you talk. Look at the way you have to beat the boys at everything. No offense, Nellie, but you're a real weirdo."

Nellie went quiet. When she spoke again, she said, "What are you scared of?"

"I ain't scared of nothing," Austin snapped. "I been runnin' around this park my whole life and never been scared. Not of buzzards or gators or snakes or — "

"I'm not talking about being scared of animals," Nellie said. "Why are you scared of me?"

"I ain't," said Austin.

"My point was that I don't have any friends here. I just thought . . . " her voice wavered. "You could be a friend. Or that you could put your stupid pride away for one minute and tell me everything's going to be okay. Maybe even give me a hug?"

"A hug?" Austin said.

Nellie's eyes were watery and red when they met Austin's. "Is that too much ask?" she said.

"How about a handshake?" said Austin.

Nellie buried her face in her hands. Her shoulders began to heave.

"Okay, okay," said Austin. "But let's get this straight. Let's get this straight right now. I'm *not* going to be your boyfriend."

Austin's first mistake was that he leaned in for the hug. His second mistake was not paying close attention. Nellie did reach to hug him. At the last second, she dropped her outstretched arms. The punch landed hard in his gut.

Austin wheezed and crumbled.

"Boy," Nellie said, "I used to think you were the stupidest boy in town." She paused. "But now it's confirmed. You just won the trophy for the stupidest boy on the planet."

Austin would have responded if he could have.

Nellie wasn't about to wait around for him to catch his breath. She had a snake to rescue.

CHAPTER NINE

OUT ON A LIMB

Austin finally regained his feet from Nellie's punch. She was long gone. He looked around. Thankfully, it seemed no one noticed that Nellie had clocked him.

From his dad's office, he grabbed a headlamp and a pair knee-high rubber boots. He also grabbed a set of long snake-handling gloves and what looked like a long garbage picker, but with a pincher at the end.

Austin looked at the pinchers and thought of Ethan's gator obsession. "Chomp, chomp," he whispered to himself. He pulled up his rain jacket's hood and headed out into the gathering darkness.

About a half-mile up along the creek, Austin heard the barking. Even with all the wind blowing and the rain, Austin recognized the sound of Bubba.

When he got within another twenty yards, he could see Hobie and Hunter standing at the foot of an old cypress that draped over the flooding river.

Hunter had a fishing pole, but he wasn't casting it toward rushing the water. He kept letting it fly up towards the tree branches.

"Just you wait, Bubba," Hobie was saying. "We're gonna fish that mean old snake down, and then we'll cut it up and feed it to you for dinner."

Austin looked up into the branches. One branch wasn't swaying at all. It was slithering. It was Red!

Hunter had some white and fuzzy lure tied to his hook. He kept getting the thing snagged up in the Spanish moss that draped the branches. The Spanish moss was gray and ghostly, and it swayed in the rain and the wind. With Hunter tugging on the snagged line, it was like the whole tree was alive.

"Be careful now," Hobie said. "Don't go knockin' chiggers all over us in the process."

"Don't be such a baby," Hunter said, leaning his body against the pole for support as he tugged away. "It's just a few bugs. Better than what I'll give you if you don't help me get this stupid thing down."

Well, Austin told himself, shaking his head. *It's time to take care of this.* "Snake pinchers?" he whispered. "Check." Then he slipped on his gloves. "Snake-handlin' gloves? Check."

He pulled the hood of his raincoat over his head until he could only see the ground below him. He fastened the headband of his headlamp. "My fire-breathing third eye? Check!"

By the time Austin lunged for the Manleys, he looked like a monster. He waved the snake pinchers.

Bubba howled. Hobie stumbled as he tried to get away as fast as he could. Hunter was right behind.

The Manleys left their fishing pole dangling from the tree branch. As they crashed through the brush, Austin pushed back his hood and laughed.

The next sound he heard made *him* jump.

"Sorry if I scared you," somebody said.

Austin looked up. A smirk lit up Nellie's face. He coughed and pretended his heart wasn't racing.

"Look up," he said. "Your snake is in the tree!"

Nellie looked up to see Red still perched in the the cypress. Pine needles and bits of Spanish moss fell into the rushing creek below whenever Red moved.

Austin knew that if Red fell in, they'd never see her again. She'd be swept away. He was already running for the tree when Nellie realized his plan.

"Don't climb that tree!" Nellie hollered. "You're too big. You'll snap the branches before you even get out to her."

Austin didn't slow down or look back. Over his shoulder, he yelled, "That's why we're gonna have to work together."

Austin pulled off his gloves and stripped out of his rain slicker before he even go to the base of the tree. He kicked off his rubber boots as well. *No excess weight*, he told himself. Nothing but him and the tree and a snake.

He reached for the lowest branch and hauled himself up. Pine needles and rough bark dug into his skin. He kept climbing anyway.

"Hold on, Red," Nellie called from the bank. "We're coming to get you, girl."

Austin reached the base of Red's branch. He didn't want to look down. He knew below him the river was rushing and roaring. His whole body screamed from the itch of chigger bites and scraped skin.

"Now what?" Nellie said from below.

"You any good at catching?" Austin said. He laid himself on the branch belly-first. The branch dipped under his weight.

Nellie said, "If you mean, like, a baseball, the answer is not really."

"We have one chance," Austin said. "Get ready." He reached out with one arm while trying to keep from falling. The entire tree seemed to shake.

CHAPTER TEN

K-I-S-S-S

Austin stretched. At the tips of his fingers, he felt the snake's tail. "Come on, Red," he hissed.

It was like the snake heard him. Red wriggled forward. Austin was able to close his hand around her tail. The scales were slick to his touch.

Austin grunted, "Open your hands, Nellie."

For maybe the first time, Nellie listened to him.

Austin knew he couldn't just drop Red. He'd need to toss her. He took aim, gently swinging the snake like a dangling rope. Then he let go.

Red somersaulted through the air. Austin had not made a perfect throw, but at the last second Nellie adjusted her position and lunged.

Nellie made the catch. "Got her!" she shouted.

Austin let out a breath he didn't know he had been holding. He inched back down the tree.

Nellie showed her gratitude by punching Austin in the shoulder. "You might be the stupidest boy I've ever met, Austin Finch," she said.

Austin said, "Told you I ain't afraid of your snake."

"Prove it," said Nellie. "Red wants a kiss."

Austin laughed, but Nellie was serious. She offered Red's face to Austin like a flower. Austin gulped.

"What?" said Nellie. "Scared of being friends?"

Without thinking, Austin put his face up to the snake. He closed his eyes, fully expecting the worst. He heard a faint hiss, then Red's tongue flicked against his nose. Austin jumped back.

Nellie laughed and wrapped Red around her neck like a scarf. She hopped on the Manley's four-wheeler. "Don't stand there like an idiot," she said. "Hop on."

Austin slid onto the four-wheeler behind her. It was hard to hear through the rain, but he was pretty sure she muttered something before she fired the motor. It almost sounded like, "Thank you."

Two weeks later was the grand opening of the Bog Hollow Snake Information and Education Exhibit.

Austin and Nellie's grounding ended just in time.

"Who knew so many folks wanted to see snakes?" said Ms. Finch, driving the boys into a full parking lot.

Under the shade of the pavilion, Bud and Willie had helped Miss Denise set up her smoker. She had a set of tongs clutched in one fist and a grilling fork in the other. She snapped her tongs on Daryl's fingers when he tried to sneak a hotlink.

"It's about time y'all showed up," Miss Denise called. "This one is workin' on my last nerve. If I catch him tryin' to poach one more of my hotlinks, he won't have no more little piggies left."

Daryl grinned guiltily.

Compared to outside, the snake education center was dark and cool. So dark, Austin bumped into a tank with a hissing three-foot eastern Indigo. He jumped.

"Making friends already, eh?" Nellie asked.

Austin hadn't seen Nellie. As his eyes adjusted to the dark, he saw Dr. Tibbits and Ranger Finch, too.

"Don't worry," Nellie said, "Indigos are harmless."

"Not like gators!" shouted Ethan. He moved his arms like alligator jaws.

"Say what you will, but I'll take a corn snake over that weirdo bro of yours any day," Nellie told Austin.

"Careful, Nellie," Ranger Finch said, approaching. "Might be a day down the road where you inherit a weirdo little stepbrother." He turned to Austin. "Might even be a day you inherit a weirdo stepsister."

If Austin could have morphed into an eagle right then, he would have. He would have flown far away from what he knew was coming next. And if Nellie could have morphed into a corn snake, she would have burrowed down into a deep dark hole.

"Whaddaya say?" Ranger Finch said to Dr. Tibbits. "Time to tell them?"

Everyone, Ranger Finch included, jumped five feet in the air when they heard Ms. Finch come up.

"Would y'all hurry it up already?" Ms. Finch said. "Miss Denise's been slaving over the smoker all day." But then she winked.

Austin had never seen his mama wink.

"Well, then," Ranger Finch said. "Let's eat."

"Yeah!" shouted Ethan. "We're all a big family!"

"Nope," Austin said. "Nothin's changed." He turned to Nellie. "And let's get a little something

straight — even if our parents are dating, I won't ever need or ask for your help. You got me?"

"Fine," Nellie said. "Long as you understand that I'll never stop beating you or making you look bad just 'cuz your dad had to go and fall in love with my mom."

"That's enough from you two," said Dr. Tibbits. She linked her arm through Ranger Finch's and took a deep breath. "Ready?"

"Ready," said Ranger Finch. He pushed open the door, and all of them walked into the hot sun, where everyone else was waiting.

ABOUT THE AUTHOR

C.B. Jones is a transplanted Southerner who came from the Northern Great Lakes area. When not teaching collegiate writing courses, Jones spends time writing love poems and adventure novels, feeding the dog, and setting bone-crushing picks in pick-up basketball games. Other bemusements include Civil War artifact hunting, spelunking, and checkers.

ABOUT THE ILLUSTRATOR

Chris Green is an Australian artist known for creating quirky characters. He has a strong love for bad jokes, great coffee, and all things related to beards. When he isn't illustrating for film or print, you might find him re-inventing the wheel with his 3D printer, playing with power tools in the shed, binge-watching television shows, or spending time with his lovely wife and their wonderful circle of friends.

GLOSSARY

ADRENALIN — a hormone produced in the body when excited that makes the heart beat faster and prepares the body for action

AVIARY — a house for birds

CHIGGERS — the parasitic larva of various mites which cause intense itching on the human skin

EXTENSIVE — covering a large area

HERPETOLOGIST — one who studies amphibians and reptiles

MORPH — change smoothly from one thing to another

MUZZLE — an animal's nose, mouth, and jaws

MULE — a small locomotive used for towing

RECONVENE — to meet again for a second time

SAUNA — a steam bath in which the steam is made by throwi water on hot stones

SPANISH MOSS — a type of American plant that has lon strands that hang down from the branches of trees

TERRARIUM — a glass or plastic container for housing land animals

YAHOO — a rude, noisy, or violent person

CORN SNAKE

lieve it or not, you can consider yourself lucky if a corn snake slither by. Corn snakes are most active ...day, but they are also shy animals that will hide under bark, ...ks to avoid being seen by humans.

...ng

...are corn snakes uncommon sights, they can be beautiful ...he snakes, which can grow up to five and a half feet ...riety of different colors and patterns. Some corn

...gray ...rd Corn Snakes, are pure white. Others, called ...kes, are light yellow with dark yellow stripes. ...ing is red or dark yellow with black-edged

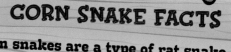
CORN SNAKE FACTS

→ Corn snakes are a type of rat snake and found in the southeastern United States.

→ Corn snakes can be red, orange, yellow, pink, light gray, lavender, or even white.

→ Snakes are not social animals. They prefer to live by themselves.

→ Corn snakes can live for up to 20 years in captivity.

→ The favorite food of a corn snake is a live mouse, which it squeezes to death and eats head first.

→ In the wild, corn snakes only eat every 2-3 days; in captivity, they can go about 8 days without feeding.

→ Corn snakes are the most popular snake to keep as a pet.

Corn Snake

THE ADVENTURE DOESN'T STOP HERE!

READ ALL THE
BOG HOLLOW BOYS
BOOKS AND FOLLOW
THE MISCHIEF!

DISCOVER MORE AT
WWW.CAPSTONEKIDS.COM